D0313665

MR.PERFECT

MR.PERFECT

by Roger Hargreaves

It was a perfect summer's day.

And on this perfect summer's day,
Mr Perfect was looking even more perfect
than usual.

He didn't have a hair out of place.

Mr Perfect lived in Tiptop Cottage.

And on this perfect summer's day,
his house was also looking even more
perfect than usual.

Not a curtain out of place.

I suppose you're wondering why
Tiptop Cottage was looking so perfect?

I shall tell you.

It was Mr Perfect's birthday,
and he was going to have a party.

There was a knock at the door.
"Perfect!" cried Mr Perfect.

"How very kind of you," he said, when he saw
that all his guests had brought wonderful
looking presents.
"Please do come in, and if no one minds,
we'll open the presents later."

Nobody minded in the least.

Well almost nobody.

"WHAT'S THAT?" roared Mr Uppity.

"I don't have any time to waste, you know!
You'd better make sure we
don't get bored today!"

Do you think this upset Mr Perfect?

Of course not.

Mr Perfect had perfect manners,
unlike rude Mr Uppity.

"Oh no, my dear Mr Uppity,
we shan't be bored today," he replied.
"First of all we shall dance."

And everybody danced.

Even Mr Uppity.

But although he danced, Mr Uppity
couldn't manage a smile.

Unfortunately, Mr Clumsy,
being his usual clumsy self,
broke a pile of plates.

Do you think this upset Mr Perfect?

Not at all!

"Don't worry, Mr Clumsy," said Mr Perfect.

And, being the perfect person he was,
and not in the least bit clumsy,
he produced a whole lot more plates …

… made of cardboard!

Then, he brought in a cake.

It was huge.

It looked wonderful.

It smelt terrific.

And …

Mr Greedy thought it tasted delicious.

He gobbled up the whole cake
in three seconds flat!

There wasn't a crumb left for anybody else!

Do you think this upset Mr Perfect?

Not in the least.

Being perfect, he had already guessed
what would happen.

Quickly, he brought out lots of small cakes.

There were plenty for everybody.

Even Mr Perfect.

But as he was not greedy, he only ate one.

One cake was just perfect for him.

Once everything had been eaten,
Mr Perfect opened his presents.

He said as many thank-yous as
there were presents.

Well, not quite.

"What about my present?" cried Mr Mean.

Mr Mean's parcel was so small that
Mr Perfect had not seen it!

Mr Perfect opened the tiny parcel,
wrapped in newspaper.

"Oh, Mr Mean," said Mr Perfect.
"You've given me a lump of coal.
How kind of you!
It's delightful!"

"If I'd known, I'd only have given him
half a lump," grumbled Mr Mean.

"THAT'S IT! I've had enough!"
cried Mr Uppity, suddenly.

"I'm fed up with you, Mr Perfect. And do you
know why? I'll tell you! I have discovered
that there is a most enormous, unbearable,
exasperating fault with you."

"Would you be so kind as to tell me what
that might be?" asked Mr Perfect,
as politely as ever.

"Don't you understand?" cried Mr Uppity.
"Your fault is …

… that you have NO faults!"